This igloo book belongs to:

....

Contents

igloobooks

Published in 2016
by Igloo Books Ltd
Cottage Farm
Sywell
NN6 0BJ
www.igloobooks.com

LEO002 0816
2 4 6 8 10 9 7 5 3 1
ISBN 978-1-78557-635-5

Written by
Diana Manning
Cheryl Hawkinson
Molly Wigand

Illustrated by Mike Esberg

Cover designed by Richard Sykes
Edited by Helen Catt

Printed and manufactured in China

Snowtime Stories

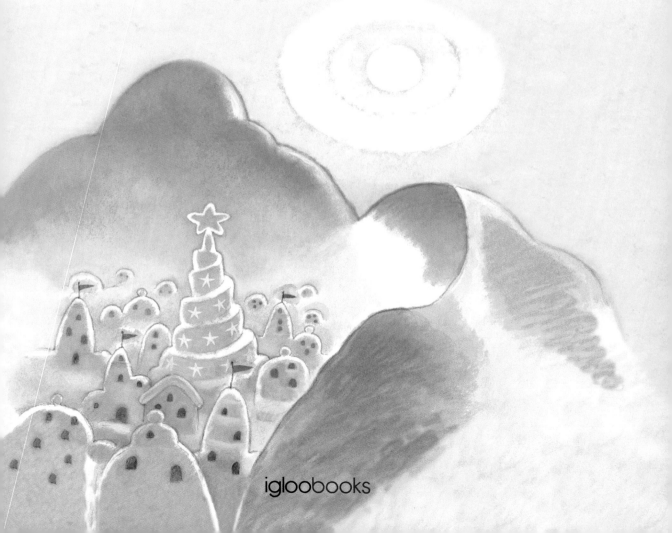

igloobooks

The Snowman Band of Snowboggle Bend

In the far northern village of Snowboggle Bend,
it snowed… and it snowed… and it snowed without end.
Snow floated and fluttered and silenced the land,
except for the sound of the town's only band.

SNOW
ROUTE

From a broken-down school bus their music came soaring,
awakening animals who'd rather be snoring.
They called themselves Snow Pack, these talented four,
and they practised and practised
and practised some more.

Snow-Joe blew sweetly on his alto sax,
while Snow-Freddy's fingers flew over his axe.

Snow-Tom on trumpet could make a horn sing,
and Snow-Ken on keys was a beautiful thing.

There was just one small problem. No one knew they existed.
It was hard to get gigs, but Snow Pack persisted.
Each year they made tracks to a nearby big city,
to audition for Slush Fest. The results were not pretty.
Each year, they received a "Sorry, but no!"
from the concert's promoter, Sir Farley Fitz Snow.

"We've got to do something," said Snow-Ken at last.
"Let's just GO to the Slush Fest. It might be a blast!"
"But how do we get there?" said Snow-Joe with a frown.
"The Snow Dome Pavilion is way out of town."
"Well, our bus is no help," sadly answered Snow-Freddy,
"Its get-up is gone and it's hardly road-ready."

"There's someone," said Snow-Tom,
"who might fix it for us.
She's quite the mechanic, my sister, Snow-Agnes."

"I'll fix it," Sis said, soon after arriving.
"But when I'm all finished, then I'll do the driving!"

So Snow Pack left town with some rattling and creaking,
but at the first curve they heard shouting and shrieking.
A huge crowd had gathered by the mountain Pass Ranch.
The band cried out loudly, "Oh no! Avalanche!"
"No one can move! Everyone's stuck!"
"Goodbye, good old Slush Fest. Man, what bad luck!"

"But where are the mammoths?" demanded Snow-Joe.
"Our town's team of woollies should shovel this snow!"
Sure enough, the two mammoths showed up at the scene,
but they wouldn't budge. They were moody and mean.

"Hey," said Snow-Freddy, "no one's leaving here soon.
We've got an audience, let's play 'em some tunes."

So they turned up their amps and they really got swinging,
and soon EVERYBODY was clapping and singing.

Then someone said "Look, the mammoths are movin'!
Who knew they liked music? They really are groovin'!"
Sure enough, the two woollies were smiling and dancing.
You would think they were reindeer
the way they were prancing.

Then quick as a flash the two creatures had cleared
a path through the mountains and everyone cheered!
When who should appear but Sir Farley Fitz Snow,
saying, "Good job, you guys. What a band! What a show!"

"This is rather last-minute but what do you say?
Could you be the star act at the Slush Fest today?"

They all looked at each other, then replied with a grin,
"Well, we are kind of busy, but we'll fit you in."

Snow Time to Lose

In the village of Shiverdale, Finny O'Flurry
is somebody everyone knows.
He's a likable snow-guy whose little dog,
Rex, is with him wherever he goes.

Now, Rex has a habit of getting in trouble.
He really does WANT to be good,
though sometimes the way that he tries to help out just
doesn't turn out like it should.

Finny is patient and brings him along
when he goes to rehearsal each week,
where he sings with his pals in the Shiverdale chorus.
Their music is really unique!

The chorus is known for the Christmas Eve
Singalong held every year on the square.
Snow-kids and snow-families join in the singing,
and everyone wants to be there!

"It's a Christmas tradition for folks far and near,"
their director says, proud as can be.
"It's a very big deal, so let's be at our best.
We've got to make sure we're on key!"

When practice begins, Finny sings from the heart,
while his little dog, Rex, really HOWLS.
Stopping the music, the stern Mr Trebleclef
grumpily grumbles and scowls.

"That dog has to go!" he finally declares,
and throws his baton in the street.
But Rex thinks they're playing a fun game of fetch,
and carries it back in his teeth.

Patting his head, Finny sends him on home,
with the promise of treats later on.
Mr Trebleclef sighs as he turns to his chorus
and takes up his icy baton.

"We've got to be ready! Our honoured guest
soloists both will be joining us soon!
Snowphie Soprano and Baron von Yodel,
arriving by hot-air balloon!"

The journey turns out to be freezy and breezy.
Poor Snowphie holds on to her hat.
Von Yodel looks over their flight plan again,
so he can make sure where they're at.

They land on the roof of Trebleclef's house
where they'll stay as his holiday guests.
"We're honoured to have you!" They're greeted
with smiles. "Won't you come in and just rest?

The very next day, when it's time for the
Singalong, Trebleclef's nowhere around.
Finny and Rex go to knock on his door and find
icicles down to the ground!

Poor Mr Trebleclef's trapped in his house,
along with the soloists, too.
"Our hot-air balloon must have melted the snow!
Now what are we going to do?"

"We've got to get out," Mr Trebleclef shouts.
"We can't disappoint all our fans!"
Soon everyone hears of their icy dilemma
and comes to help out with a plan.

They try to break through, but the ice is too thick
and they wonder what they should do next,
when Finny O'Flurry declares, "Not to worry!"
and calls for his little dog, Rex.

Popping his head from a snow bank nearby,
the lovable Rex reappears.
"Not HIM again," Trebleclef loudly protests.
"That dog has been trouble for YEARS!"

Then Finny starts singing, with Rex joining in
with an ear-splitting howl of a sound.
It rattles the ground and they hear a big CRACK!
as the icicles all tumble down!

"There's no time to lose!" Mr Trebleclef shouts.
"The Singalong's ready to start!"
So he and the soloists rush to the square,
while already singing their parts.

The Shiverdale Singalong happens as planned
and everyone's really relieved.
The crowd gives a cheer and surrounds Rex and Finny
as heroes who saved Christmas Eve!

The Snow Must Go On

The sun shone bright in the South Pole sky as the snow-people and penguins of Antarctic Springs prepared for Christmas. Shoppers hunted for perfect surprises, children made wishes and everyone decorated the town's shimmering ice-tree. December feels cool and crisp at the bottom of the world, but warmth and goodwill bustled in the tiny snow-covered town.

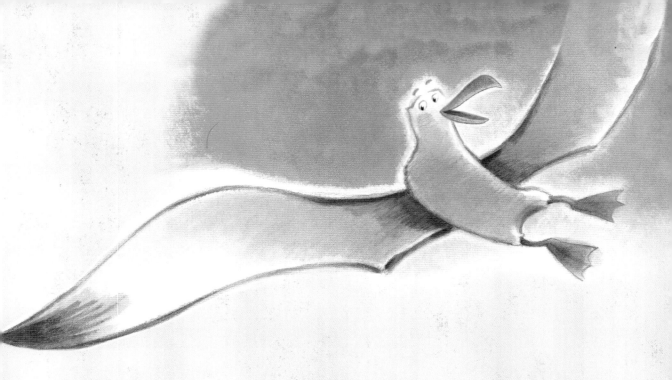

At midday, a silver speck appeared in the eastern sky.
It grew larger and larger until...
"It's the albatross!" yelled a snowman.
The bird flapped over the town square, casting dusky shadows
against the sparkling snow. "Come one, come all!" squawked
the albatross. "Mayor Flakely has called a town meeting.
It's urgent! Meet in the square at moonrise!"

That evening, every snowman and woman, every snow-kid, every snow-dog and cat, and every penguin, great and small, hurried to the square. "Welcome, citizens!" boomed Mayor Flakely, a tall, distinguished snowman. "It's December again. Children everywhere are thinking about one particular wintry wonderland. The marvellous place where Christmas begins…"

"You mean the North Pole?" asked a tiny penguin.

The mayor nodded. "Yes, the North Pole," he sighed.

SOUTH POLE

"Wouldn't it be nice if people knew that South Pole folk are also merry? If only there was some way to show the world how jolly we can be! Does anyone have any good ideas?" said Mayor Flakely.

The albatross raised his wing. "How about a cool slogan? Like, um, 'The South Pole. Ice, and lots of it.'"

"Maybe we could offer a fancy cruise," suggested a snow-mum. Mayor Flakely scratched his head. "Hmm… cruises and icebergs? That's not a good fit."

A group of penguins jumped up and down excitedly.
"We know!" they giggled. "Pick us! Pick us!"
"What is it, little friends?" asked the mayor.
"Let's put on a show!" they yelled.
And just like that, it was settled. Antarctic Springs
would put on the biggest, best Christmas show
ever, to show the world that the South Pole
could be just as fun as the North Pole.

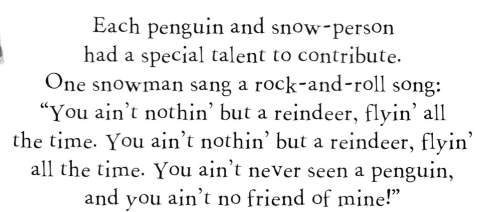

Each penguin and snow-person
had a special talent to contribute.
One snowman sang a rock-and-roll song:
"You ain't nothin' but a reindeer, flyin' all
the time. You ain't nothin' but a reindeer, flyin'
all the time. You ain't never seen a penguin,
and you ain't no friend of mine!"

Another snowman practised a magic trick.
"Watch me pull a penguin out of my hat!
Nothing up my sleeve! Presto!"
The penguin squirmed in the snowman's mitten.
"Ouch!" yelled the penguin.
"Watch the feathers, Buster!"

Strains of "The Nutcracker Suite" filled the air over the town's skating rink. Five young penguins twirled to the music. "Point your flippers," said the teacher. "Look pretty now. It's 'Waltz of the Flowers!' Be a flower!"

"What's a flower?" asked one of the penguins.

Another penguin brought a big kettle to the town square.
"I will now juggle fifteen fish with my foot flippers," he
boasted. One at a time, he added fish to his juggling show.
"And... behind the back!" he continued.
"Blindfolded! Ta-dah!"

A big, burly comedian used a stick for a microphone.
"So a snowman walks into an ice-cream shop.
The shopkeeper says, 'Go away. We're closed.'
Snowman says, 'C'mon. Let me in! I'm an Ice-Guy!' Get it?
An! Ice! Guy! Nice Guy! Is this thing on?" the comedian joked,
tapping the microphone stick with his hand.
"Whoa. Chilly room."

Before long, the songs were in tune, the dancers were in step and the finishing touches were put on a magnificent theatre in the valley. The mayor gathered the cast and crew backstage for a final meeting before the show.
"You know what's wonderful about this show?" he asked.
"Every person in town has joined in! Soon, the world will know how jolly we can be!"

As everybody cheered, a tiny snow-girl raised her hand. "If everyone's in the show," she asked, "who's going to watch it?" Stillness blanketed the crowd.

"Shhh! Did you hear that jingle-jangle?" asked a penguin. "And the prancing and pawing?" added a snow-dog.

HO! HO! HO!

The cast peeked through the curtain. Right there, in the front row, all the way from the North Pole, was Santa himself with all his reindeers. The cast performed their hearts out. The show was a smash hit!
"Bravo, South Pole!" yelled Santa. "You've proven that North, South, East or West, it's the joy in our hearts that counts at Christmas!" And at that magical moment, in that tiny Antarctic town, everyone felt on top of the world.